There's An Apple In Daddy's Eyes!

Shola Johnson

To order additional copies of this book, contact:
Xlibris
844-714-8691
www.Xlibris.com
Orders@Xlibris.com

ISBN: Softcover   978-1-4535-9702-6
        Hardcover   978-1-4535-9703-3
        EBook   978-1-6698-3005-4

Library of Congress Control Number: 2010915766

Print information available on the last page

Rev. date: 06/13/2022

This book is dedicated to my wonderful son, Remi. Who is the treasure of my life, the golden nugget at the foot of my rainbow.

There are no words to express the love and adoration I have for you. Daddy has such great hopes for you, my son. My head is

filled with big dreams of the promise that you have brought into my life. I hope you would read great books, embark on multiple

adventures, study hard, get good grades, be filled with talents and quick on your feet. Love exploration and forge meaningful

friendships. I hope that you would be good with your hands and fassil with your mind. I hope that you would have a penchant

for math and science, and develop the charm and charisma that would draw people to you.

But the thing I hope for the most above all else is that you practice Simplicity, humility, nobility, generosity, integrity, Sincerity and Responsibility.

There's an apple in daddy's eyes!

An apple, sweet or sour fresh or

seasoned.

Teach your child at a very early age

about the virtues of eye contact.

All children must learn to say: Please!

Thank you! and Nice to meet you.

There's an apple in daddy's eyes!
An apple that blossoms and ripens
through sunrise and sundown.

Have civilized conversations with your
child, even if they are too young to
understand. Talk about current events,
politics, mythology, religion, music,
sports, travel, toys and of course school.

8

There's an apple in daddy's eyes!
An apple, canned, juiced, dipped in
syrup and coated in caramel.

Respect your child's individuality.
Always knock before you enter her
room. Never call her names. Be an
attentive parent and actually listen to
what she has to say. Value her opinion,
honor your commitments and never,
ever, tell her a lie.

There's an apple in daddy's eyes!

An apple, smooth and rich, crisp and

crunchy.

Encourage your child to question

authority. Help them think for

themselves. After all, it was you who

told him to stand up for what he

believes in.

There's an apple in daddy's eyes!

An apple, rich in Choline and calcium, potassium and phosphorus.

Whenever your child is confused about something, tell her to take some time to figure out a good resolution. Then, assist her in figuring out what that resolution might be.

There's an apple in daddy's eyes!

An apple, filled with fiber and folate,

healthy and tasty.

Have high expectations of your child. It

would definitely pay off in the long run.

There's an apple in daddy's eyes!

But this apple...

It's not red or green or colors in between.

Help your child build a magical imagination. Ask her what she would do if she ruled the world.

It's not forested or fermented but still leave your lips lamenting.

Never choose sides. Never play favorites. Never criticize your child and never, ever yell.

It's not apple sauce or apple pie but step right up and give it a try.

Hugs and kisses are a must. Always hug and kiss your child everyday the sun rises.

It's not Mcintosh or Melrose but

still delicious enough to warrant a

megadose.

Live everyday with your child as though

it is your last day on earth.

APPLE ALPHABET

It's Not...

Austin

Baldwin Woodier

Cortland

Detroit Red

Empire

Fuji

GrannySmith

Honey CrispGala

Ida Red

Jazz

Keepsake

LeatherCoat

Mcintosh

NorthernSpy

Olween

PinkLady

Queen Cox

Red Delicious

Seek-No-Further

Twenty Ounce

Ultra Red Gala

Victory

Whitney Crab

Xavier De Bavay

York Imperial

Zestar

It's not...

Austin

Baldwin Woodier

Cortland

Detroit Red

Empire

Fuji

Granny Smith

Honey CrispGala

Ida Red

Jazz

Keepsake

Leather Coat

McIntos

Northern

Olween

Pink Lady

Queen Cox

Red Delicious

Seek-No-Further

Twenty Ounce

Ultra Red Gala

Victory

Whitney Crab

Xavier De Bavay

York Imperial

Zestar

There are hundreds of varieties of
apples around the world,

but only one can boast of being
"The apple in daddy's eyes."

So what is the apple in daddy's eyes you might ask?

The apple in daddy's eyes is...

You!

I love you son.

The End

Printed in the United States
by Baker & Taylor Publisher Services